ILLUSTRATED CLASSICS

# Sleeping Beauty

## AND OTHER CLASSIC TALES

AF807496

*COMPILED BY*

PATRICIA MOORE

NEW DELHI (INDIA)

ILLUSTRATED CLASSICS

# Sleeping Beauty

AND OTHER CLASSIC TALES

Concept, layout and design © MAANU GRAPHICS

*Published by*

MG BOOKS

*An Imprint of*

MAANU GRAPHICS

**MAANU GRAPHICS**

**(PUBLISHERS OF GENERAL BOOKS)**

5FF, Ganpati Bhawan, 21 Ansari Road,
Darya Ganj, New Delhi-110002
Ph: 65285220, 64138266
E-mail : maanugraphics@yahoo.com
mgbooks.maanu@yahoo.com

No part of this publication may be reproduced, stored in any retrieval system, or transmitted in any form or by any means, electronic, mechanical, photocopying, recording or otherwise, without prior permission of the author.

*Printed at :*
Satyam Enterprises, Delhi

## CONTENTS

*A Feast for the Fairies*

# SLEEPING BEAUTY

There were formerly a King and a Queen, who were so sorry that they had no children; so sorry that it cannot be expressed. They went to all the waters in the world; voyages, pilgrimages, all ways were tried, and all to no purpose.

At last, however, the Queen had a daughter. There was a very fine christening; and the Princess had for her godmothers all the fairies they could find in the whole kingdom (they found seven), that every one of them might give her a gift, as was the custom of fairies in those days. By this means the Princess had all the perfections imaginable.

After the ceremonies of the christening were over, all the company returned to the King's palace, where was prepared a great

*Behind the Wall Hangings*

feast for the fairies. There was placed before every one of them a magnificent cover with a case of massive gold, wherein were a spoon, knife, and fork, all of pure gold set with diamonds and rubies. But as they were all sitting down at table they saw come into the hall a very old fairy, whom they had not invited, because it was about fifty years since she had been out of a certain tower, and she was believed to be either dead or enchanted.

The King ordered her a cover, but could not furnish her with a case of gold as the others, because they had only seven for the seven fairies. The old fairy fancied she was slighted, and muttered some threats between her teeth. One of the young fairies who sat by her overheard how she grumbled; and, judging that she might give the little Princess some unlucky gift, went, as soon as they rose from table, and hid herself behind the wall hangings, that she might speak last, and repair, as much as she could, the evil which the old fairy might intend.

In the meanwhile all the fairies began to give their gifts to the Princess. The youngest gave her for a gift that she should be the most beautiful person in the world; the next, that

*"I am Spinning, My Child."*

she should have the wit of an angel; the third, that she should have a wonderful grace in everything she did; the fourth, that she should dance perfectly; the fifth, that she should sing like a nightingale; and the sixth, that she should play all kinds of music to the utmost perfection.

The old fairy's turn coming next, with a head shaking more with spite than age, she said that the Princess should have her hand pierced with a spindle and die of the wound. This terrible gift made the whole company tremble, and everybody fell a-crying.

At this very instant the young fairy came out from behind the hangings, and spoke these words aloud:

"Assure yourselves, O King and Queen, that your daughter shall not die of this disaster. It is true, I have no power to undo entirely what my elder has done. The Princess shall indeed pierce her hand with a spindle; but, instead of dying, she shall only fall into a profound sleep, which shall last a hundred years, at the expiration of which a King's son shall come and awake her."

The King, to avoid the misfortune foretold by the old fairy, immediately caused a proclamation to be made, whereby everybody was forbidden, on pain of death, to spin with a distaff and spindle, or to have so much as any spindle in their houses.

About fifteen or sixteen years later, the King and Queen being gone to one of their other castles, the young Princess happened one day to divert herself by running up and down the palace; when going up from one apartment to another, she came into a little room on the top of the tower, where a good old woman, alone, was spinning with her spindle. This good woman had never heard of the King's proclamation against spindles.

"What are you doing there, goody?" said the Princess.

"I am spinning, my pretty child," said the old woman, who did not know who she was.

"Ha!" said the Princess, "this is very nice; how do you do it? Give it to me, that I may see if I can do so."

She had no sooner taken it into her hand than, whether being very hasty at it, somewhat unhandy, or that the decree of the fairy had so ordained it, it ran into her hand, and she fell down in a swoon.

The good old woman, not knowing very well what to do in this affair, cried out for help. People came in from every quarter in great numbers; they threw water upon the Princess's face, unlaced her, struck her on the palms of her hands, and rubbed her temples with water; but nothing would bring her to herself.

And now the King, who had come back, bethought himself of the prediction of the fairies, and, judging very well that this must necessarily come to pass, since the fairies had said it, caused the Princess to be carried into the finest apartment in his palace, and to be laid upon a bed all embroidered with gold and silver.

One would have taken her for a little angel, she was so very beautiful; for her swooning away had not diminished one bit of her complexion: her cheeks were carnation, and her lips were coral; indeed her eyes were shut, but she was heard to breathe softly, which satisfied those about her that she was not

*A Bed All Embroidered in Silver and Gold*

dead. The King commanded that they should not disturb her, but let her sleep quietly till her hour of awaking was come.

The good fairy who had saved her life by condemning her to sleep a hundred years was in the kingdom of Matakin, twelve thousand leagues off, when this accident befell the Princess; but she was instantly informed of it by a little dwarf, who had boots of seven leagues, that is, boots with which he could tread over seven leagues of ground in one stride. The fairy came away immediately, and she arrived, about an hour after, in a fiery chariot drawn by dragons.

The King handed her out of the chariot, and she approved everything he had done; but as she had very great foresight, she thought when the Princess should awake she might not know what to do with herself, being all alone in this old palace; and this was what the good fairy did: she touched with her wand everything in the palace (except the King and the Queen) – governesses, maids of honor, ladies of the bedchamber, gentlemen, officers, stewards, cooks, undercooks, scullions, guards, pages, footmen; she likewise touched all the horses which were in the stables, the

*Touched with Her Wand*

great dogs in the outward court and pretty little Mopsey too, the Princess's little spaniel, which lay by her on the bed.

Immediately upon her touching them, they all fell asleep, that they might not awake before their mistress, and that they might be ready to wait upon her when she wanted them. The very spits at the fire, as full as they could hold of partridges and pheasants, did fall asleep also. All this was done in a moment. Fairies are not long in doing their business.

And now the King and the Queen, having kissed their dear child without waking her, went out of the palace and put forth a proclamation that nobody should dare to come near it.

This, however, was not necessary, for in a quarter of an hour's time there grew up all round about the park such a vast number of trees, great and small, bushes and brambles, having one within another, that neither man nor beast could pass through; so that nothing could be seen but the very top of the towers of the palace, and then, not unless one was a good way off.

Nobody doubted that the fairy gave herein a very extraordinary sample of her art, that the Princess, while she continued sleeping, might have nothing to fear from any curious people.

When a hundred years were gone and passed, the son of the King then reigning, who was of another family from that of the sleeping Princess, being gone a-hunting on that side of the country, asked:

What were those towers which he saw in the middle of a great thick wood?

Everyone answered according as they had heard. Some said:

That it was a ruinous old castle, haunted by spirits;

Others: that all the sorcerers and witches of the country kept there their night's meeting.

The common opinion was that an ogre lived there, and that he carried there all the little children he could catch, that he might eat them up at his leisure, without anybody being able to follow him, as only he had the power to pass through the wood.

The Prince did not know what to believe, when a very aged countryman spoke to him thus:

"May it please your royal highness, it is now about fifty years since I heard from my father, who heard my grandfather say, that there was then in this castle a Princess, the most beautiful ever seen; that she must sleep there a hundred years, and should be awakened by a King's son, for whom she was reserved."

The young Prince was all on fire at these words, believing, without weighing the matter, that he could put an end to this rare adventure; and, pushed on by love and honor, resolved that moment to look into it.

Scarce had he advanced towards the wood when all the great trees, the bushes, and brambles gave way of themselves to let him pass through; he walked up to the castle which he saw at the end of a large avenue and he entered it.

What surprised him was that he saw none of his people could follow him, because the trees closed again as soon as he had passed through them. However, he did not cease

*What Were Those Towers?*

from continuing his way; a young and gallant Prince is always valiant.

He came into a spacious outward court, where everything he saw might have frozen up the most fearless person with horror. There reigned over all a most frightful silence, with nothing to be seen but stretched out bodies of men and animals, all seeming to be dead. He, however, very well knew that they were only asleep; and their goblets, in which still remained some drops of wine, showed plainly that they fell asleep as they drank.

He then crossed a court paved with marble, went up the stairs, and came into the guard chamber, where guards were standing in their ranks, with their muskets upon their shoulders, and snoring as loud as they could.

After that he went through several rooms full of gentlemen and ladies, all asleep, some standing, others sitting.

At last he came into a chamber outfitted with gold and silver, where he saw upon a bed, the curtains of which were all open, the finest sight was ever beheld – a Princess, whose bright and, in a manner, resplendent beauty seemed somewhat divine. He

*Pushed On By Love and Honour*

approached with trembling and admiration, and fell down before her upon his knees.

And now, as the enchantment was at an end, the Princess awoke, and looking on him with eyes more tender than imaginable, asked:

"Is it you, my Prince? You have waited a long while."

The Prince, charmed with these words, and much more with the manner in which they were spoken, knew not how to show his joy and gratitude; he assured her that he loved her better than he did himself; their discourse was not well connected, they did weep more than talk – little eloquence, but a great deal of love.

He was more at a loss than she, and we need not wonder at it: she had time to think on what to say to him; for it is very probable (though history mentions nothing of it) that the good fairy, during so long a sleep, had given her very agreeable dreams. In short, they talked four hours together, and yet they said not half what they had to say.

*"You Have Waited a Long Time."*

In the meanwhile all the palace awoke; everyone thought upon their particular business, and as all of them were not in love, they were ready to die of hunger. The chief lady of honor, being as sharp set as other folks, grew very impatient, and told the Princess aloud that supper was served.

The Prince helped the Princess to rise; she was dressed very magnificently, but his royal highness took care not to tell her that she was dressed like his great grandmother; she looked not a bit the less charming and beautiful for all that.

They went into the great hall of mirrors, where they supped, and were served by the Princess's officers; the violins and oboes played old tunes, but very excellent, though it was now a hundred years since they had played; and after supper, without losing any time, the lord almoner married them in the chapel of the castle, and they lived happily together, perhaps even for another hundred years!

*"Please Spare My Home."*

# THE THREE WISHES

Once upon a time in a deep, dark forest there lived a poor woodsman and his wife. Every day the woodsman went out to cut down trees to make timber, and every day the work became more difficult to do.

Early one morning, after his wife had packed a meager lunch for him to take along, the woodsman started off. He went deep, deep into the forest, looking for a tree to provide him with a goodly amount of wood.

At last he spotted a great oak tree. This will make a fine day's work for me, thought the woodsman. He took his ax in both hands, swinging it over his head as he prepared to chop down the tree.

But as the ax began to descend, he heard a small voice that seemed to come from within

*"Make Your Wishes with Care."*

the tree itself.

The woodsman paused in amazement, the ax stopped in midair. "Please, please, sir," came the voice, "do not cut down this tree, kind woodsman, please spare me my home."

The woodsman's wonder grew as from out of the very tree itself there appeared a beautiful little spirit, standing in front of him.

The spirit repeated its plea and the woodsman, dumbfounded, at last nodded his head in agreement.

"I will do as you wish, little spirit," he said slowly, "even though it means the loss to me of a good day's work and wages."

"In doing goodness to me, I will do more than goodness to you," replied the spirit. "To show you how appreciative I am of your goodness and kindness, I will make magic for you. I will grant you the fulfillment of your next three wishes, whatsoever it may be that you wish for."

The spirit rose in the air slightly, its wings hovering, as it reached out its hand to touch the woodsman on both his shoulders. "Go now, kind man, and make your wishes with care and good thought."

The spirit disappeared, almost melting into the air, as mysteriously as it had come. The woodsman stood still for a few minutes, thoroughly dazed by all he had seen and heard. At last he recovered his senses, gathered his belongings about him, and started off through the forest for home.

As he trudged on home, his mind was full of the wonderful events of the day. He rubbed his head, wondering whether he had really seen the spirit of the tree, or if it had been a vision, or perhaps even just a dream.

All of this thinking and questioning was far more thought than he was used to, and by the time the poor woodsman found himself at his own doorstep, he was thoroughly exhausted.

He went inside, wanting nothing but the comfort of his wife, his fire, and a good hot dinner.

"My, but you're home much too early for dinner to be done!" exclaimed his wife. "It lacks a good two hours before the food will be ready."

"Ah me, I wish I had a good sausage right now!" he replied.

All at once, right in front of the woodsman appeared a platter in which was sizzhng as brown and perfect a sausage as he or anybody else in the world could wish for.

"How now! What is this?" asked his wife, rushing over as the fragrance of the spicy meat filled all the corners of their little house. "Where in the world did it come from?" she asked again in amazement.

It was then that the poor woodsman remembered his meeting with the spirit of the tree, and the magic that granted him his first three wishes.

"What have I done, what have I done?" the poor man groaned, holding his head in his fists. "I'd completely forgotten, and now one of my magic wishes is wasted!"

"What magic? What wishes?" his wife demanded, not understanding any of it.

It was then that he collected his senses, remembering it all, and telling her everything that had happened that afternoon.

*"Good Sausage Right Now!"*

The wife listened quietly at first, scarcely believing her ears. But when she realized that one wish had already been wasted on the foolish sausage, her anger knew no limits.

"What have you done, what have you done?" she wailed over and over again, standing over her husband, waving her arms about as though she were going to strike him. "Look at this stupid sausage!" she exclaimed. "This is what you wished for when you might have gotten us all of the gold we could ever need for the rest of our lives, or a fine new house instead of this poor shack, or a coach and horses to drive us back and forth from the town whenever we wished?"

"I know, I know," the old man moaned, "but I was so hungry, all I could think of was something to eat. That's why I asked for the sausage."

"Sausage! Sausage indeed!" his wife shouted. "I wish the sausage was hanging from the tip of your nose right now!"

No sooner had the words left her mouth than the sausage, as if it could fly, rose up from the platter and attached itself exactly

*"From the Tip of Your Nose!"*

where she had wished it to be.

"Oh no, wife, oh no!" the old man cried. "Now look at what you've done!"

He started tugging at the sausage, trying to get it loose, but it was no use. Even when his wife added her hands to his, they could not move the sausage, not even a fraction of an inch.

The man looked up at his wife. "You know what it will take to remove it," he said, pleading with his voice and his eyes. "You know there will be only one way."

The wife bit her lip, and nodded. It was clear to both of them that only the third wish would be strong enough to remove the sausage from the end of the poor woodsman's nose.

The wife cocked her head, looking sharply at her husband. "You know," she said slowly, staring at him all the while, "if you look at it from a certain angle, it really doesn't look so bad at all. I warrant you would get used to it in very little time."

"Oh no, wife!" exclaimed the woodsman. "You can't be thinking that! You can't be

*Not That Bad from a Certain Angle*

wanting me to stay like this for the rest of my life!"

"You could get used to it," his wife said insistently. "Many folk have had to put up with much worse."

The poor man was beside himself. He knew that his wife wanted to save the third wish for one of her grand ideas. But what good would all that grandness be to him, he thought, if he were to spend the rest of his life in such a condition?

With all the strength he could summon, the poor woodsman shouted, "I wish this terrible thing was off my nose!"

Quick as a wink, there was the sausage once more, sizzling in the platter and sending forth the most delicious fragrances.

So there were no bags of gold, no horse-drawn carriages, no lofty palace for the poor woodsman and his wife. But, at least, for the day's adventure, they sat down to as fine a meal as had ever been served them!

*The Prince Bent Down.*

# THE FLOWER QUEEN'S DAUGHTER

A young Prince was riding one day through a meadow that stretched for miles in front of him, when he came to a deep open ditch. He was turning aside to avoid it, when he heard the sound of someone crying within it. He dismounted from his horse, and stepped along in the direction the sound came from. To his astonishment he found an old woman, who begged him to help her out of the ditch. The Prince bent down and lifted her out of her living grave, asking her at the same time how she had managed to get there.

"My son," answered the old woman, "I am a very poor woman, and soon after midnight I set out for the neighboring town in order to sell my eggs in the market on the following morning; but I lost my way in the dark, and

*"You are a Mighty Prince."*

fell into this deep ditch, where I might have remained forever but for your kindness."

Then the Prince said to her, "You can hardly walk; I will put you on my horse and lead you home. Where do you live?"

"Over there, at the edge of the forest in the little hut you see in the distance," replied the old woman.

The Prince lifted her on to his horse, and soon they reached the hut, where the old woman got down, and turning to the Prince said, "Just wait a moment, and I will give you something." And she disappeared into her hut, but returned very soon and said, "You are a mighty Prince, but at the same time you have a kind heart, which deserves to be rewarded. Would you like to have the most beautiful woman in the world for your wife?"

"Most certainly I would," replied the Prince.

So the old woman continued, "The most beautiful woman in the whole world is the daughter of the Queen of the Flowers, who has been captured by a dragon. If you wish to marry her, you must first set her free, and

*He Came to a Hut.*

this I will help you to do. I will give you this little bell: if you ring it once, the King of the Eagles will appear; if you ring it twice, the King of the Foxes will come to you; and if you ring it three times, you will see the King of the Fishes by your side. These will help you if you are in any difficulty. Now farewell, and heaven prosper your undertaking." She handed him the little bell, and hut and all disappeared, as though the earth had swallowed them up.

Then it dawned on the Prince that he had been speaking to a good fairy, and putting the little bell carefully in his pocket, he rode home and told his father that he meant to set free the daughter of the Flower Queen, and intended setting out on the following day into the wide world in search of her.

So the next morning the Prince mounted his fine horse and left his home. He had roamed round the world for a whole year, and his horse had died of exhaustion, while he himself had suffered much from want and misery, but still he had come on no trace of her he was in search of. At last one day he came to a hut, in front of which sat a very old man. The Prince asked him, "Do you not know

*Seven Dragons Rushed on Him!*

where the Dragon lives who keeps the daughter of the Flower Queen prisoner?"

"No, I do not," answered the old man. "But if you go straight along this road for a year, you will reach a hut where my father lives, and possibly he may be able to tell you,"

The Prince thanked him for his information, and continued his journey for a whole year along the same road, and at the end of it came to the little hut, where he found a very, very old man. He asked him the same question, and the old man answered, "No, I do not know where the Dragon lives. But go straight along this road for another year, and you will come to a hut in which my father lives. I know he can tell you."

And so the Prince wandered on for another year, always on the same road, and at last reached the hut where he found the third old man.

He put the same question to him as he had put to his son and grandson; but this time the old man answered, "The Dragon lives up there on the mountain, and he has just begun his year of sleep. For one whole year he is always awake, and the next he sleeps. But if

*The Prince Undertook the Task.*

you wish to see the Flower Queen's daughter go up the second mountain: the Dragon's old mother lives there, and she has a ball every night, to which the Flower Queen's daughter goes regularly."

So the Prince went up the second mountain, where he found a castle all made of gold with diamond windows. He opened the big gate leading into the courtyard, and was just going to walk in, when seven dragons rushed on him and asked him what he wanted!

The Prince replied, "I have heard so much of the beauty and kindness of the Dragon's Mother, and would like to enter her service."

This flattering speech pleased the dragons, and the eldest of them said, "Well, you may come with me, and I will take you to the Mother Dragon."

They entered the castle and walked through twelve splendid halls, all made of gold and diamonds. In the twelfth room they found the Mother Dragon seated on a diamond throne. She was the ugliest woman under the sun, and, added to it all, she had three heads.

Her appearance was a great shock to the Prince, and so was her voice, which was like the croaking of many ravens. She asked him, "Why have you come here?"

The Prince answered at once, "I have heard so much of your beauty and kindness, that I would very much like to enter your service."

"Very well," said the Mother Dragon; "but if you wish to enter my service, you must first lead my mare out to the meadow and look after her for three days; but if you don't bring her home safely every evening, we will eat you up."

The Prince undertook the task and led the mare out to the meadow. But no sooner had they reached the grass than she vanished. The Prince sought for her in vain, and at last in despair sat down on a big stone and contemplated his sad fate. As he sat thus lost in thought, he noticed an eagle flying over his head. Then he suddenly bethought him of his little bell, and taking it out of his pocket he rang it once. In a moment he heard a rustling sound in the air beside him, and the King of the Eagles sank at his feet.

"I know what you want of me," the bird said. "You are looking for the Mother Dragon's mare who is galloping about among the clouds. I will summon all the eagles of the air together, and order them to catch the mare and bring her to you." And with these words the King of the Eagles flew away.

Towards evening the Prince heard a mighty rushing sound in the air, and when he looked up he saw thousands of eagles driving the mare before them. They sank at his feet on to the ground and gave the mare over to him.

Then the Prince rode home to the old Mother Dragon, who was full of wonder when she saw him, and said, "You have succeeded today in looking after my mare, and as a reward you shall come to my ball tonight." She gave him at the same time a cloak made of copper, and led him to a big room where several young he-dragons and she-dragons were dancing together.

Here, too, was the Flower Queen's beautiful daughter. Her dress was woven out of the most lovely flowers in the world, and her complexion was like lilies and roses. As the

*"I Have Come to Set You Free!"*

Prince was dancing with her he managed to whisper in her ear, "I have come to set you free!"

Then the beautiful girl said to him, "If you succeed in bringing the mare back safely the third day, ask the Mother Dragon to give you a foal of the mare as a reward."

The ball came to an end at midnight, and early next morning the Prince again led the Mother Dragon's mare out into the meadow. But again she vanished before his eyes. Then he took out his little bell and rang it twice.

In a moment the King of the Foxes stood before him and said, "I know already what you want, and will summon all the foxes of the world together to find the mare who has hidden herself in a hill."

With these words the King of the Foxes disappeared, and in the evening many thousand foxes brought the mare to the Prince.

Then he rode home to the Mother Dragon, from whom he received this time a cloak made of silver, and again she led him to the ballroom.

*The King of the Fishes Appeared.*

The Flower Queen's daughter was delighted to see him safe and sound, and when they were dancing together she whispered in his ear, "If you succeed again tomorrow, wait for me with the foal in the meadow. After the ball we will fly away together."

On the third day the Prince led the mare to the meadow again; but once more she vanished before his eyes. Then the Prince took out his little bell and rang it three times.

In a moment the King of the Fishes appeared, and said to him, "I know quite well what you want me to do, and I will summon all the fishes of the sea together, and tell them to bring you back the mare, who is hiding herself in a river."

Towards evening the mare was returned to him, and when he led her home to the Mother Dragon, she said to him,

"You are a brave youth, and I will make you my body servant. But what shall I give you as a reward to begin with?"

The Prince begged for a foal of the mare, which the Mother Dragon at once gave him, and over and above, a cloak made of gold, for she had fallen in love with him because he had praised her beauty.

In the evening he appeared at the ball in his golden cloak; but before the entertainment was over he slipped away, and went straight to the stables, where he mounted his foal and rode out into the meadow to wait for the Flower Queen's daughter. Towards midnight the beautiful girl appeared, and placing her in front of him on his horse, they flew like the wind till they reached the Flower Queen's dwelling.

But the dragons had noticed their flight, and woke their brother out of his year's sleep. He flew into a terrible rage when he heard what had happened, and determined to lay siege to the Flower Queen's palace; but the Queen caused a forest of flowers as high as the sky to grow up round her dwelling, through which no one could force a way.

When the Flower Queen heard that her daughter wanted to marry the Prince, she said to him, "I will give my consent to your marriage gladly, but my daughter can only stay with you in summer. In winter, when everything is dead and the ground covered with snow, she must come and live with me in my palace underground."

The Prince consented to this, and led his beautiful bride home, where the wedding was held with great pomp and magnificence. The young couple lived happily together till winter came, when the Flower Queen's daughter departed and went home to her mother.

In summer she returned to her husband, and their life of joy and happiness began again, and lasted till the approach of winter, when the Flower Queen's daughter went back again to her mother. This coming and going continued all her life long, and in spite of it they always lived happily together.

*Here Sat a Duck on Her Nest.*

# THE UGLY DUCKLING

It was a glorious day in the country. It was summer, the cornfields were yellow, the oats green, the hay had been put up in the green meadows, and the stork went about on his long red legs and chattered in Egyptian, the language he had learned from his mother. All around the fields and meadows were great forests, and in the midst of the forests were deep lakes.

In the midst of the sunshine lay an old farm, with deep canals, and from the wall down to the water grew great hedges, so high that little children could stand upright under the tallest of them. It was just as wild there as in the deepest wood.

Here sat a duck on her nest to hatch her ducklings. She was already tired even before

*"The Largest Egg Still Lies There."*

the little ones came; and she seldom had visitors. The other ducks preferred to swim about rather than sit down under a hedge to gossip with her.

At last one eggshell after another burst open. "Peep! Peep!" they cried, and soon in all the eggs there were little creatures that stuck out their heads.

"Quack! quack!" they said, and they all came quacking out as fast as they could, looking all round them at the green leaves. Their mother let them look as much as they chose, for green is good for the eye.

"How big the world is!" said all the ducklings, for they certainly had much more room now than when they were in the eggs.

"D'ye think this is all the world?" said the mother. "That stretch goes far across the other side of the garden, into the parson's field; I have never even been there yet. I hope you are all here," and she stood up. "No, not all. The largest egg still lies there. How long is that to last? I am really tired." And she sat down again.

"Well, how goes it?" asked an old duck who had come to pay her a visit.

*Can It Be a Turkey Chick?*

"It's taking a long time with this one egg," said the mother duck. "It will not burst. Now, only look at the others. Are they not the prettiest little ducks one could possibly see? They are all like their father; the rogue never comes to see me."

"Let me see the egg which will not burst," said the old visitor. "You may be sure it is a turkey's egg. I was once cheated in that way, and had much trouble with the young ones, for they are afraid of the water. I could not get them to venture in. I quacked and I clacked, but it was no use. Let me see the egg. Yes, that's a turkey's egg. Let it lie there and go teach the other children to swim."

"I think I will sit on it a little longer," said the duck. "I've sat so long now that I can sit a few days more."

"Just as you please," said the old duck; and away she went.

At last the great egg burst. "Peep! peep!" said the little one, and crept forth. It was very large and ugly. The duck looked at it.

"It's a very large duckling," said she, "none of the others look like that: can it really

*"No, it's not a turkey"*

be a turkey chick? Well, we shall soon find out. It must go into the water, even if I have to thrust it in myself."

The next day it was bright, beautiful weather; the sun shone on all the green trees. The mother duck went down to the canal with all her family. Splash! She jumped into the water. "Quack! quack!" she said, and one duckling after another plunged in. The water closed over their heads, but they came up in an instant, and swam; their legs went of themselves, and they were all in the water. The ugly gray duckling swam with them.

"No, it's not a turkey," said the mother, "look how well it can use its legs, and how straight it holds itself. It is my own child! On the whole it's quite pretty, if one looks at it rightly. Quack! quack! Come with me, and I'll lead you out into the great world, and present you in the duck yard; but keep close to me, so that no one may tread on you; and take care of the cats!"

And so they came into the duck yard. There was a terrible riot going on in there, for two families were quarreling about an eel's head, and the cat got it after all.

*It Became Worse and Worse.*

"See, that's how it goes in the world!" said the mother duck; and she whetted her beak, for she too wanted the eel's head. "Only use your legs," she said. "See that you all bustle about, and bow your heads before the old duck yonder. She's the grandest of all here; she's of royal blood – that's why she's so fat; and d'ye see? She has a red rag round her leg; that's something particularly fine, and the greatest distinction a duck can enjoy; it signifies that one does not want to lose her, and that she's to be known by animals and by men, too.

Shake yourselves, don't turn in your toes; a well-brought-up duck turns its toes quite out, just like – so! Now bend your necks and say 'Quack!' "

And they did so: but the other ducks round about looked at them, and said quite boldly – "Look there! Now we're to have these hanging on, as if there were not enough of us already! And how that duckling yonder looks; we won't stand that!" And one duck flew up at it, and bit it in the neck.

"Let it alone," said the mother; "it does no harm to anyone."

"Yes, but it's too large and peculiar," said the duck who had bitten it; "and therefore it must be put down."

"Those are pretty children that the mother has there," said the old duck with the rag round her leg. "They're all pretty but that one; that was rather unlucky. I wish she could bear it over again."

"That cannot be done, my lady," replied the mother duck. "It is not pretty, but it has a really good disposition, and swims as well as any other; yes, I may even say, it swims better. I think it will grow up pretty, and become smaller in time; it has lain too long in the egg, and therefore is not properly shaped."

And then she pinched it in the neck, and smoothed its feathers. "Moreover it is a drake," she said. "I think he will be very strong: he makes his way already."

"The other ducklings are graceful enough," said the old duck. "Make yourself at home, and if you find an eel's head, you may bring it to me."

And now they were at home. But the poor

duckling which had crept last out of the egg, and looked so ugly, was bitten and pushed and jeered, as much by the ducks as by the chickens.

"It is too big!" they all said. And the turkey-cock, who had been born with spurs, and therefore thought himself an emperor, blew himself up like a ship in full sail, and bore straight down upon it; then he gobbled and grew quite red in the face.

The poor duckling did not know where it should stand or walk; it was quite melancholy because it looked ugly, and was the butt of the whole duck yard.

So it went on the first day, and afterwards it became worse and worse. The poor duckling was hunted about by everyone; even its brothers and sisters were quite angry with it, and said, "If the cat would only catch you, you ugly creature!" And the mother said, "If you were only far away!" and the ducks bit it, and the chickens beat it, and the girl who had to feed the poultry kicked at it with her foot.

Then it ran and flew over the fence, and the little birds in the bushes flew up in fear.

*The Wild Ducks Flew Up.*

"That is because I am so ugly!" thought the duckling. It shut its eyes, but flew on farther; and so it came out into the great moor, where the wild ducks lived. Here it lay the whole night long, and it was weary and downcast.

Toward morning the wild ducks flew up, and looked at their new companion.

"What sort of a one are you?" they asked, and the duckling turned in every direction, and bowed as well as it could. "You are remarkably ugly!" said the wild ducks. "But that is nothing to us."

Poor thing! It only hoped to obtain leave to lie among the reeds and drink some of the swamp water.

Thus it lay two whole days; then there came two wild ganders. It was not long since each had crept out of an egg, and that's why they were so saucy.

"Listen, comrade," said one of them. "You're so ugly that I like you. Will you go with us, and become a bird of passage? Near here, in another moor, there are a few sweet lovely wild geese, all unmarried, and all able to say, 'Rap.' You've a chance of making your fortune, ugly as you are."

"Piff! paff!" resounded through the air; and the two ganders fell down dead in the swamp, and the water became blood red. "Piff! paff!" it sounded again, and the whole flock of wild geese rose up from the reeds. A great hunt was going on. The sportsmen were all round the moor, some even sitting in the trees. Blue smoke rose up among the trees, and wafted across the water; the hunting dogs came into the swamp, and bent the rushes and reeds.

That frightened the poor duckling! It turned its head under its wing; but at that moment a frightful dog stood close by. His tongue hung out of his mouth, and his eyes gleamed; he thrust out his nose close to the duckling, showed his sharp teeth and away he went, without touching it.

"Oh, thank heaven!" said the duckling. "I am so ugly even a dog does not like me!"

It lay quiet, while gun after gun fired. Late in the day, all was still; the poor duckling did not dare rise, but waited several hours before it hastened out of the moor as fast as it could. It ran on and on, but there was such a raging storm that it was difficult to get anywhere.

The duck came to a miserable little hut, so dilapidated that it did not itself know on which side to fall; that's why it stood. The storm raged around the duckling so that the poor creature had to sit down, to stand it; the wind blew worse and worse. The duckling saw that the hinges of the door had given way, and the door hung so that the duckling could slip through the crack and into the room.

Here lived a woman, with cat and hen. And the cat, whom she called Flixx, could arch his back and purr, and give out sparks; but for that one had to stroke his fur the wrong way. The hen had short legs, and she was called Little Biddie; she laid good eggs, and the woman loved her well.

In the morning the strange duckling was spotted at once, causing the cat to purr and the hen to cluck.

"What's this?" said the woman. She thought the duckling was a fine catch. "This one is a prize! I hope to have duck's eggs."

The duckling was on trial for three weeks; but no eggs came. The cat was master of the house, and the hen the lady, and they always said, "We and the world!" for they thought

*Frightful Dog Stood Close By*

they were half the world, and the better half by far. The duckling might have a different opinion, but the hen would not permit that.

"Can you lay eggs?" she asked.

"No."

"Then hold your tongue!"

And the cat said, "Can you curve your back, or give out sparks?"

"No," said the duckling, who sat sadly in a corner.

But when the fresh air and warm sunshine streamed in, it was seized with a strong longing to swim, and could not help telling the hen about it.

"What can you be thinking?" cried the hen. "You have nothing to do, that's why you dream of things. Lay eggs, purr, or do something useful and it will pass."

"But to swim on the water," said the duckling wistfully, "to let it flow over one's head, and to dive to the bottom."

"I fancy you must have gone crazy," said the hen.

*The Cat Was Master; the Hen the Lady*

"You don't understand me," said the duckling. "I think I will go out into the wide world."

"Yes, do," replied the hen.

So the duckling went. It swam and dove, but it was snubbed by everyone because of its looks.

Soon it was autumn. The leaves turned gold and red and brown; the wind caught them about, and the air was very cold. The clouds hung heavy with hail and snow. The poor little duckling watched one evening as there came a flock of great, handsome birds, white, with long, flexible necks: swans.

They spread their great wings, and flew away from that cold region to warmer lands, to fair open lakes. They mounted high and the ugly duckling felt strange as it watched them. It turned in the water like a wheel, stretched its neck toward them, and uttered strange cries, loud and longing.

Then it could see them no longer and it dived down and when it came up again, it was quite sad. It knew not those birds, nor whither they flew; but it loved them more

*There Came a Flock of Great, Handsome Birds*

than it had ever thought to have loved any one.

The winter grew very cold. The duckling would swim about in the water, but every night the hole in which it swam became smaller. It froze so hard that the icy covering crackled, and the duckling used its legs continually to keep the hole from entirely freezing. At last it was too exhausted, and lay quite still, and froze into the ice.

The next morning a peasant passing by saw what had happened. He broke the ice and carried the duckling home. Then it came to life again. The children wanted to play, but the duckling thought they wanted to hurt it, and in its terror the poor creature slipped out into the snow where it lay exhausted.

It lay among the reeds until the sun began to shine and it was beautiful spring once again.

All at once the duckling could flap its wings, and more strongly than before, and before it knew how it happened, it found itself in a great garden, where the willows bent their long green branches down to the stream.

*The Duckling Could Flap Its Wings Again*

From the thicket there came three white swans; they rustled their wings, and swam on the water. The duckling remembered the splendid creatures, and felt a peculiar sadness.

"I will fly to them and they will beat me, because I dare to come near them. Better am I to be killed by *them* than by ducks, and fowls, and pushed about by the girl who cares for the poultry yard, and to suffer in winter!"

It flew out into the water, and swam toward the beautiful swans who looked at it, and came sailing with outspread wings. "Kill me!" said the poor creature, and bent its head down upon the water, expecting its death.

But what it saw in the clear water was its own image; and no longer was it a clumsy bird, ugly and hateful to look at, but a swan!

It felt quite glad now as the great swans swam around it, and stroked it.

In the garden little children threw bread and corn seeds into the water, and cried, "There is a new one!" and they shouted joyously, "Yes, a new one has arrived!" They clapped their hands and ran to their parents;

*The Most Beautiful of all!*

now bread and cake were thrown into the water: "The new one is the most beautiful of all! So young and handsome!" they said, and the old swans bowed to him.

He felt quite ashamed, his head under his wings, and did not know what to do, he was so happy. He had been persecuted; now he heard them saying he was most beautiful of all the birds. Even the willow bent its branches into the water before him, and the sun shone warm and mild. Then he lifted his slender neck, and cried rejoicingly from the depths of his heart, "I never dreamed of so much happiness when I was the ugly duckling!"

*Each in a Different Direction*

# THE THREE LITTLE PIGS

Once upon a time there were three little pigs who lived with their mother. One day, she decided it was time for her three sons to go out on their own.

She gathered them to her. "Listen, my children," she said, "you are all of an age to make your own ways in the world.

Go with my blessing and always remember this: beware of wolves. They are our enemies and they can do you much harm."

The three little pigs packed up their belongings and each went off in a different direction.

The first little pig was walking along his chosen road when he met a man hitching large piles of hay. The little pig had an idea. "This

*I'll Huff and I'll Puff!*

must be my lucky day, I can build my house of hay!"

He gave the man some of the coins his mother had tucked carefully into his pouch, and off he went to build his house.

The little pig worked very hard and at last the house was done. He had just settled in to have a nice cup of tea when he heard a terrible noise outside.

It was a wolf!

"Little pig, little pig, let me come in!"

"Not by the hair of my chinny chin chin,"

cried the little pig.

"Then I'll huff and I'll puff

and I'll blow your house in!"

yelled the wolf.

He huffed and he puffed and in one great breath, the wolf blew down the little house of hay.

The little pig ran out as quickly as he could, and went to look for his brothers.

The second little pig was walking along a road when he met a man who had a great wagon load of wood.

"This is something very good,

I think I'll build my house of wood!"

said the little pig.

He paid the man for the whole wagonload of wood and set off to build his house.

The little pig liked his house of sturdy sticks, and he settled in to enjoy himself.

But it wasn't long before he heard a terrible howling outside his window.

"Little pig, little pig,

let me come in!"

called the wolf.

"Not by the hair of my chinny chin chin!"

cried out the little pig.

"Then I'll huff and puff

and I'll blow your house in!"

called the wolf.

He huffed and he puffed and he puffed and he huffed and at last the little house of wood fell all to pieces.

The little pig ran away as fast as he could to look for his brothers.

The third little pig was on his way when he saw a man with a great load of bricks.

"I'll have walls so safe and thick

if I build my house of brick!"

thought the third little pig.

He carted off the whole load of bricks and worked very carefully to build his big, strong house.

And just in time! For here came his two brothers, running quickly from opposite directions. The strong brick house was big enough for all of them, and the three little pigs settled in very happily.

The third little pig had just put up a big kettle of soup for their dinner when from outside came such a howling and rumbling that even the windowpanes of the sturdy brick house shook.

*And I'll Blow Your House In!*

"Little pigs, little pigs,
let me come in!"
shouted the wolf.

"Not by the hairs of our chinny chin chins!"
shouted back the pigs.

"Then I'll huff and I'll puff
and I'll blow your house in!"
shouted the wolf.

He huffed and he puffed and he puffed and he huffed and he puffed and he huffed some more, but the wolf could not blow down the sturdy brick house!

The wolf was getting very angry. He knew that the three little pigs were safe inside. He could not blow down the house of bricks. He had to think of something else.

The wolf looked around carefully. He saw the chimney on top of the house. "Ah ha," he thought, "I can climb up there. Then I'll slide down the chimney and be inside the house."

It was very quiet, and the three little pigs thought that the wolf had gone away. But then

*Wolf Soup!*

they heard a scampering, scratching sound above them. They knew the wolf was on the roof.

The third little pig stirred and stoked the fire under the big kettle. Soon he had a roaring blaze going. That would make a warm welcome indeed for the big bad wolf!

Soon enough, down came the wolf. Right into the boiling kettle he went.

And what do you think the three little pigs had for supper that night? Wolf soup! Plus, with no big bad wolf to bother them anymore, the three little pigs lived happily ever after.

*The Marble Figure from the Wreck*

# THE LITTLE MERMAID

Where the sea is deepest lies the palace of the Ocean King, who had been a widower many years. His old mother managed his household affairs for him, particularly her grand-daughters, the little Ocean Princesses. They were six beautiful children; the youngest Princess, however, was the loveliest of all, but, like all mermaids, she had no feet, her body ending in a tail like a fish.

In front of the palace was a large garden where each of the little Princesses had her own flower bed which she could plant as she liked. One laid hers out in the form of a whale, another liked that of a mermaid better; but the youngest made hers quite round, like the sun, and planted in it only flowers that were red, to resemble it in color, too. She was an extraordinary child, very quiet and thoughtful. While her sisters were adorning themselves with all sorts of things as ornaments, which they had got from a ship that had been wrecked, she asked only for the beautiful marble figure of a boy which had been found in the vessel. She placed this statue in her garden, and planted a red weeping willow beside it.

Nothing delighted the little Princess so much as to hear of the world above the waters. Her old grandmother would tell all that she knew about ships and towns, men and land-animals.

"When you have reached your fifteenth year," said the old lady, "you may rise up to the surface of the sea, sit in the moonlight, and see the large ships sail by, and become acquainted with men and cities."

The following year the eldest sister would attain this happy age; but as to her sisters, unfortunately one was always a year younger than the other, and the youngest had to wait five whole years before the glad moment should come for her to rise and behold how the upper world did look.

Each promised the others to tell what she had seen, and what she thought most beautiful, for really their grandmother told them so very little, and there were so many things that they wanted to know; besides what she told them only excited their curiosity to see the wonders with their own eyes.

But none of the sisters felt so lively a longing for this day as the youngest; she who must wait longest, and who always was so quietly absorbed in thought. Many a night she stood at the open window, and look upwards through the clear blue water, while the fishes were splashing and playing around her.

She could see the sun and the moon, in dimmed brightness only; but to her they seemed larger than they do to dwellers on earth. If a shadow concealed them, she knew that it was either a whale or a passing ship with human beings upon it, who certainly little thought that, far below, a little ocean-maiden stretched her hands upwards towards the keel of their ship, with an ardent longing to be with them.

The day now arrived when the oldest Princess reached her fifteenth year, and was to rise to the surface of the sea.

*Nothing Delighted the Little Princess So Much*

At her return she had a thousand things to relate; her greatest enjoyment had been to sit on a sand-bank in the moonlight, and to see the large city on the coast, where lights like stars were shining, music sounding, and where the noise and hum of carriages and men might be heard afar. Then, too, to behold the high church towers, and to hear the chime of the bells – it was for these she felt the greatest longing, because they were beyond her reach.

How attentively did her youngest sister listen to these words! And when she next stood by night at her open window, and looked upwards through the blue flood, she thought so intensely of the great noisy city, that she fancied she could hear the sound of the church bells.

The following year the next sister rose to the surface, to swim whither she pleased. She rose to the top of the water as the sun was going down; and this sight so delighted her, that she said, of all she had seen above the sea, this was the most magnificent.

"The whole heaven was like gold," said she, "and the beauty of the clouds is out of

*A Thousand Things to Relate*

my power to describe: now red, now violet, on they sailed above me; a flock of white swans flew over the water at the very spot where the sun was descending."

It was now the third sister's turn to visit the upper world. She was the most beautiful and the boldest of the three, and swam up a river that fell into the sea. Here she saw green hills with grapevines, castles and houses among the woods; she heard the birds singing; the sun shone so warm, that she had often to dive beneath the water to cool her burning face.

In a small bay she found a whole company of little children who were bathing and jumped and splashed in the water. She wished to join them, but the children fled frightened to the land, and a little black animal barked so at her, that she grew afraid, and swam back again to the sea. But she could not forget the green woods, the leafy hills, and the little children who swam about in the water although they had no fins.

The fourth sister was not so bold; she remained in the open sea; she related that there it was more beautiful than anywhere

*The Third Sister's Turn*

else, for one could see miles around, while the sky, like a large bell, hung over the waves. She saw ships too, but so far off that they seemed to be seagulls; while sprightly dolphins sported on the water, and whales spouted high jets into the air that looked like a thousand fountains.

The next year the fifth sister was fifteen. Her birthday was in winter, and she saw what the others had not when she went up. The sea had become green, and icebergs were swimming about its surface. These looked like pearls, she said, but were higher than the church towers on the land. She had seated herself on one of these swimming ice-pearls, and let the wind play with her long hair; but every ship had quickly hoisted its sails, and had moved quickly away.

The first time that each sister rose from the sea, she was enchanted at the many new and beautiful objects she had seen in the upper world. But now, as grown-up maidens, they had permission to go up as often as they liked, and it soon lost the charm of novelty. It was not long before their own home seemed much more delightful than the upper world.

*The Five Sisters Arm-in-Arm*

Many an evening did the five sisters, arm-in-arm, rise to the surface of the sea. When they swam on the tops of the waves, the youngest remained quite alone in her father's palace, looking after them; and at such times she felt as though she could weep. But mermaids have no tears, and therefore suffer immeasurably more in their sorrow than human beings, for tears melt human sorrow.

"Oh, were I but fifteen years old!" sighed she. "I know, for certain, that I should love the upper world and the men that live upon it very dearly!"

At length her much-desired fifteenth year was here!

"Now, then, it is your turn," said the old grandmother. "Come here, that I may dress you like your sisters."

So saying, she placed a royal wreath of white lilies in her hair, whose every petal was the half of a pearl.

She would gladly have cast aside all her finery, and taken off the heavy wreath, for the red flowers of her garden became her much better; but she dared not do so before the old lady.

"Adieu," she said, and rose out of the sea as light and as beautiful as a bubble in water.

The sun had just left the horizon as the Little Mermaid, for the first time, appeared on the surface of the ocean; but the clouds still shone golden and rose-colored, the evening star gleamed in the pale sky, the air was mild and the sea as smooth as a mirror.

A large ship with three masts lay on the tranquil waters; a single sail was hoisted, for not a breath of air was perceptible and the sailors were sitting on the yards or in the rigging. Music and song sounded from on board; and when it was dark, hundreds of lamps suddenly glittered on the ship, and it looked as if the flags of every nation were fluttering in the air.

The Little Mermaid swam to the cabin-windows, where, each time the waves lifted her, she could see through the clear glass panes. Here she saw many gaily-dressed persons; but the handsomest of all was a young Prince with large dark eyes.

He was certainly not more than sixteen. It was his birthday, which accounted for all these festivities. The seamen danced on deck; and when the young Prince appeared among them, hundreds of rockets went up in the air, turning the night into bright day, and frightening the Little Mermaid so much that she plunged beneath the water for a minute or two.

But she soon peeped out again, and it now seemed as if all the stars of heaven were falling around her. Such a rain of fire she had never seen: of such arts, known but to men, she had never even dreamed. Large suns turned round, glowing fishes swam in the air, and the whole spectacle was reflected in the clear surface of the sea.

On the ship itself it was so light that one could distinguish persons distinctively – oh, how handsome the young Prince was! To many of the people he gave his hand, and joked and laughed; while the music sounded pleasantly in the silence of the night.

It was already late; however, the little Princess could not tear herself away from the sight of the ship and the handsome Prince. She remained looking through the cabin window, rocked to and fro by the waves.

*A Large Ship Lay on the Water*

But there was a roaring in the depths of the ocean, while the Princess still swam on the surface in order to see the Prince. The ship began to move more quickly, the sails were hoisted, the waves tossed, black clouds gathered over the sky, and the noise of distant thunder was heard. The sailors perceived that a storm was coming on, so they again furled the sails. Already the huge vessel rocked on the heaving sea like a mere skiff, and the waves, towering like black mountains, broke over it: but the good ship glided downwards in the hollow of the sea like a swan, and appeared again immediately riding on the crest of the waves now lashed into foam.

To the Little Mermaid this appeared very amusing: but not so to the sailors on board. The vessel creaked and groaned, and her thick ribs bent under the heavy blows of the waves against her side, while the water rushed in. For a moment the ship reeled; the main mast snapped as though it had been a reed; she capsized and filled.

Now the Little Mermaid comprehended that the people on board were in danger; for she herself was obliged to watch out for the spars and timbers that had been torn away

*How Handsome the Young Prince Was!*

from the ship and were now tossing about in all directions on the waves.

At this moment it became so dark that she could not distinguish anything; though when the dreadful lightning played, it was so light that she recognized everybody on the wreck. Her eyes sought the young Prince just at the moment when the ship went to pieces and sank.

At first she was glad, thinking the Prince would now come to her; but she immediately recollected that men cannot live in the water, and that the Prince could only reach her palace as a corpse. Die? No, that he should not!

She swam through the wreck that the waves were driving about in all directions, forgetful of her own danger, dived and rose again, till at last she reached the spot where the Prince, almost exhausted, kept himself with difficulty just above the water.

His eyes were already closing, and he would inevitably have been drowned if the Little Mermaid had not come to his rescue. But she seized hold of him, and, while she was driven along by the waves, bore him above the water.

*The Ship Reeled, the Main Mast Snapped*

Towards morning the storm abated: but no trace of the ship was to be seen. The sun rose as red as fire. Its first rays seemed to color the Prince's cheeks, but his eyes were still shut. The Little Mermaid kissed his forehead, and put back his wet hair from his face. He resembled the marble figure in her garden: she kissed him once more, and wished most fervently that he might revive, and that his eyes might open and look upon her.

Now she beheld the land with its high mountains, on which white snow was shining. A green wood stretched along the coast, and in front of it lay a chapel. The sea formed here a small bay, and the fine sand that had been washed up formed firm ground. Here the Mermaid swam with the seemingly dead Prince, and took care to turn his face towards the sun, that its warmth might call back his life.

In the large white building that stood before her, the bells began to sound, and many young maidens came out to walk in the garden.

The little Princess hid herself behind some rock, covered her head and hair with the froth of the sea that her face might not be seen, and watched carefully to see who would approach the Prince.

It was not long before one of the young girls went towards him. She seemed quite terrified at the sight of the lifeless Prince; but, soon recovering herself, she ran back to call her sisters.

The Prince revived, and smiled kindly and joyfully on all who surrounded him; but on the Little Mermaid he cast no look, for he did not know that it was to her he owed his life.

And when he was taken from where she had brought him, and carried into the large building, she grew so sad that she immediately plunged beneath the water and returned sorrowfully to her father's palace.

If she had been formerly thoughtful and quiet, she was now more so. Her sisters asked her what she had seen in the world above, but she gave no answer.

She often rose of an evening near the shore where she had left the Prince; she saw how the fruits of the garden were gathered; she saw how the snow on the mountains vanished; but the Prince she never could see;

and she always returned to her submarine dwelling melancholy and sad.

Her only consolation was to sit in her garden, and to embrace the little statue that resembled the handsome Prince; she tended her flowers no longer; they grew wild, covered the paths, and so twined their long stalks and leaves round the branches of the trees that the whole garden was turned into a gloomy bower.

At last no longer able to conceal her sorrow, she told her secret to one of her sisters. The other sisters now learned the secret and one recollected the Prince; she, too, had been a witness of festivities on board; she knew in what country he was to be found, and the name of his sovereign.

"Come, little sister!" said the other Princesses, and, twining their arms together, they rose in a line out of the sea just in front of the castle of the Prince.

Now the little Princess knew where her dear Prince lived; and she showed herself nearly every evening, and many a night on the water. She approached nearer the land

*The Little Mermaid Kissed His Forehead*

than her sisters had; she even swam the length of the narrow canal that led below the marble balcony. Here she tarried to gaze at the young Prince, who imagined himself alone in the clear moonlight.

She often saw him, too, on the water in his splendid barge, over which the many flags were flying. She listened from among the green rushes which grew on the banks, to hear his voice; and if by chance a light breeze caught her silver veil, and the fluttering was observed by those in the Prince's boat, they thought it a swan stretching out its long white wings over the water.

Many a night when the fishermen were out by torchlight, she heard them relating much good of the Prince, and the noble actions he had performed. She rejoiced greatly at having saved his life, and she remembered how his head rested on her shoulder, and how she had kissed him when he knew nothing of it, nor even dreamed of such a thing.

Dearer and dearer did the human race become to her, and more and more did she wish to belong to them. Their world seemed to her much larger than that of the sea; they

*He Was Carried Into the Large Building*

could fly away in their ships over the ocean, climb to the summits of the highest mountains that reached the clouds of heaven; and their countries, bordered by woods and decked with pleasant fields, extended themselves much father than the eye of a mermaid could reach.

There were so many things about which she would have gladly asked, but her sisters could give her no answers. So she had to have recourse to the old Queen-Mother, who was well acquainted with the upper world, which she used to call "the country above the sea."

"Does the human race live forever if the people are not drowned?" she asked her grandmother. "Do they never die, as we do who live at the bottom of the sea?"

"Yes," replied the old lady, "they must die as well as we; and besides, their lifetime is much shorter than ours. We can live to be three hundred years of age; when we die we become foam on the sea, and have not a grave here below among those we love. We have no immortal soul, we do not live again, but are like reeds that, once cut, can never more grow green. But men have a soul that lives on and

*Now She Knew Where Her Dear Prince Lived*

which soars upward to the shining stars in heaven. As we rise out of the water to see the countries of men, so do they rise to unknown abodes in the skies, which our eyes are not permitted to behold."

"Why do we not have immortal souls?" asked the Little Mermaid. "I would give all my three hundred years to be a human creature only for a day, and then to be allowed to dwell forever in the heavenly world."

"You must not think of such a thing," answered her old grandmother. "Why, we are much better off than men, and are far happier."

"And is there nothing I can do, grandmother, to obtain an immortal soul?"

"No," answered she. "Only when a mortal loves you so much that you are more to him than father and mother; when every thought and all his love is concentrated in you, and he gives his hand to the priest to be laid in yours with the promise of everlasting constancy – only then can you become immortal; for then would his soul dissolve in

*"Why Do We Not Have Immortal Souls?"*

yours, and you would be made a partaker of human happiness."

"But that can never happen! What in our eyes is the handsomest part of our bodies, the tail, is considered frightful by men because they know no better. According to them, one must have two awkward props to one's body, 'legs,' as they call them, in order to look well!"

Then the Little Mermaid sighed, and looked sorrowfully at the scaly part of her body.

"Let us be happy!" continued the old lady, "Tonight there is a ball at court."

But all the Little Mermaid's thoughts were occupied with the world above her: she could not forget the handsome Prince, and her grief at not possessing an immortal soul was very great. She stole away from her father's house; and while all within was merriment and joy, she sat absorbed in thought in her little neglected garden.

She heard the sound of horns, echoing from above through the water, far away in the distance; and she thought, "He is about to depart for the chase — he whom I love more than anything, who occupies my thoughts incessantly, and in whose hand I would gladly lay my life! All, all, will I hazard to win him and an immortal soul! I will go to the Witch of the Sea, whom I always dreaded, but who is perhaps the only one who can counsel and assist me."

The Little Mermaid went to the roaring Maelstrom, beyond which the sorceress dwelt. She had never been that way before: no flower grew along the path, nothing but the bare sandy ground extended itself to the Maelstrom, in which the water whirled and hurled all that it seized on down into the abyss. She would have to pass through the middle of this crushing whirlpool to arrive at the territory of the Witch, and a long part of the way led through boiling ooze.

Behind this lay her house, in wood of a peculiar sort, and a strange abode it was. All the trees and bushes consisted of serpents shooting up out of the earth. The branches were long shiny arms that unceasingly stretched out in every direction. What they caught in this manner they held so tight that it could never get loose again.

The Little Mermaid stood quite horrified before this frightful wood; she had nearly turned back, her mission unaccomplished, when her thoughts fell on the Prince and the immortal soul, and inspired her with new strength.

She bound up her long flying hair, that the trees might not seize it and drag her towards them, and more swiftly than a fish darts through the water, she flew safely through the fearful wood. She reached a place where large sea-snails were about; and in the middle of this place stood a house built of the bones of those who had been lost at sea. Here sat the Witch, caressing a toad in the same manner as we often see persons feeding a canary. The snails she called her chickens, and allowed them to sit upon her spongy shoulders and about her neck.

"I know well what you would ask of me," said she to the little Princess; "your intention is foolish, but your wish shall be fulfilled, my pretty maiden, though it is sure to bring misfortune on you. You would get rid of your tail, and to have in its place two stilts such as men use, that the young Prince may fall in

*The Little Mermaid Sighed*

love with you, and you may get an immortal soul.

"I will prepare you a potion, with which you must swim to the land; you must then sit on the shore, and drink it. Your fish's tail will immediately fall off, and shrivel up into what men call 'legs;' but this transformation is very painful, and you will feel as if a sharp instrument were thrust through your whole body. All who behold you will say you are the most beautiful mortal they have ever seen; you will retain your gliding gait, and no dancer, be she ever so light, will move with so elastic a step; but at every motion you will suffer intolerable pain; you will feel as though you were treading on sharp blades. If you will subject yourself to all these torments, I will grant your request."

"Yes, I will!" answered the little Princess, with trembling voice; for she thought of her beloved Prince, and of getting an immortal soul.

"But remember," said the Witch, "you can never be a mermaid again, when you have taken human form; you will never be able to descend to your sisters and your home, and should you not gain the Prince's love in such

*"I Will Go to the Witch of the Sea"*

degree that, for your sake, he forget-teth father and mother, that all his thoughts and all his joy be in you, and join your hands together as man and wife — without this you will never obtain the immortality you seek. The morning after he is united to another will be the day of your death; your heart will break for grief, and you will changed into the foam on the waves of the sea."

"I still will venture!" continued the Little Mermaid, pale and trembling like on the point of death.

"But I must be paid, too, and it is no trifle that I require of you for my trouble. You have the most charming voice of all the dwellers in the sea, and with it you reckon to captivate the Prince; but this voice I must have. The best of your possessions I demand for my miraculous potion; for I must give of my own blood to impart to the mixture the sharpness of a two-edged sword."

"But if you take my voice from me," said the Princess, "what have I left to captivate the Prince?"

"Your lovely form," answered the Witch;

"your light airy step, and your expressive eyes. These are surely enough to befool a poor human heart! Well, what do you say? Have you lost your courage? Come, that I may take it for myself in exchange for my magic drink."

"Be it so!" answered the Princess.

The Witch set her cauldron on the fire to seeth the charmed potion. "Cleanliness is a principal thing," said she, and let the blood drop into the vessel. Every moment the Witch threw in new ingredients; and when the cauldron boiled, sighs rose resembling the wail of the crocodile. At last the mixture was ready, and was transparent as pure water as she poured it into a vial.

"There it is," said the Witch to the Princess; and at the same moment she took her voice. The Little Mermaid was thus made dumb; she could neither speak nor sing.

She now looked once again at her father's palace; the lamps in the ballroom were extinguished, and all her family were doubtless gone to rest. She would not enter, as she was unable to speak, and was, besides, on the point of leaving her home forever. At the thought her heart was well-nigh broken; she glided into the garden, picked a flower from the bed of each sister as a remembrance, waved with her hand many a farewell towards the palace, and then rose through the dark blue waters to the upper world.

She reached the Prince's dwelling, and ascended the well-known marble steps. And now the Little Mermaid emptied the vial with the piercing potion, which convulsed her whole frame: she felt it pass through her like the thrust of a sword, and it affected her so that she sank lifeless on the ground.

When the sun rose she awoke, and felt a burning pain in every limb; but before her stood the object of her fervent love, the handsome young Prince, with his dark eyes upon her. She looked down and saw that, in place of her long fish-like tail the finest legs were grown.

The Prince asked who she was, and from where she came; and, smiling sweetly, she looked at him with her bright blue eyes, for she could speak no more. He then took her hand, and led her into his castle. At every step it was as the Witch had said — as though

*She Flew Through the Fearful Wood*

she was treading on sharpcutting blades; but she bore the pain willingly. She moved along beside the Prince like a zephyr; and all who saw her wondered at the charming grace and lightness of her every movement.

When she had entered the palace, robes of costly silk were handed to her, and she was the most lovely among the ladies of the court, though she could speak and sing no longer. Female musicians dressed in silk and gold brocade now came to sing before the Prince and his royal parents. One was particularly distinguished by her beautiful clear voice; and the Prince showed his approval by clapping his hands. This made the Little Mermaid quite sad, for she knew she could have sung much better if her voice had not been taken from her.

"Oh," thought she in silence, "if he did but know that for his sake I have sacrificed my voice forever!"

They now began to dance. The dainty Little Mermaid stretched out her delicate arms, and danced with such an air as had never been seen before. With every movement the lovely grace of her body seemed more apparent, and

*"You Can Never Be a Mermaid Again"*

the expression which beamed in her eyes appealed to the heart of the spectators far more movingly than the songs of the female musicians.

All present were enchanted with her, but especially the young Prince, who called her his dear little foundling. And she danced again, and more beautifully still, although at every step she was obliged to bear the cutting knives; and the Prince said she should always remain in his palace; and an apartment was prepared for her, provided with graceful furniture, and a bed of velvet cushions.

And the Prince had a riding-dress made for her, that she might accompany him on horseback; and they rode together through the fragrant woods, where the green boughs touched their shoulders, and the little birds rejoiced from behind the fresh leaves. With the Prince, too, she climbed the highest mountains; and although her delicate feet bled as she went on, so that the attendants saw it, she only smiled, and still followed her dear Prince up on high, where she saw the clouds chasing each other beneath them like a flock of birds passing to other lands.

*"Be it so!"*

At night, when all the palace was asleep, she would descend the marble steps to cool her feet in the refreshing sea; and she thought then of her dear ones in the deep.

Once, while she was standing there, her sisters came swimming by, arm-in-arm, and their singing was most melancholy. She beckoned to them, and her sisters recognized her, and told her how great had been the mourning for her in their father's house.

Henceforward they visited their sister every night, and once brought with them their old grandmother, who for many years had not been in the upper world, and their father too, the Ocean King, with the crown upon his head. But the two did not venture so near the land as to be able to speak to her.

Each day the Little Mermaid grew dearer to the Prince; he loved her like a good dear child; but to make her his wife never even entered his thoughts; and yet she must become his wife before she could obtain an immortal soul; and his wife she must be, or be changed into foam and be driven restlessly and forever over the billows of the sea.

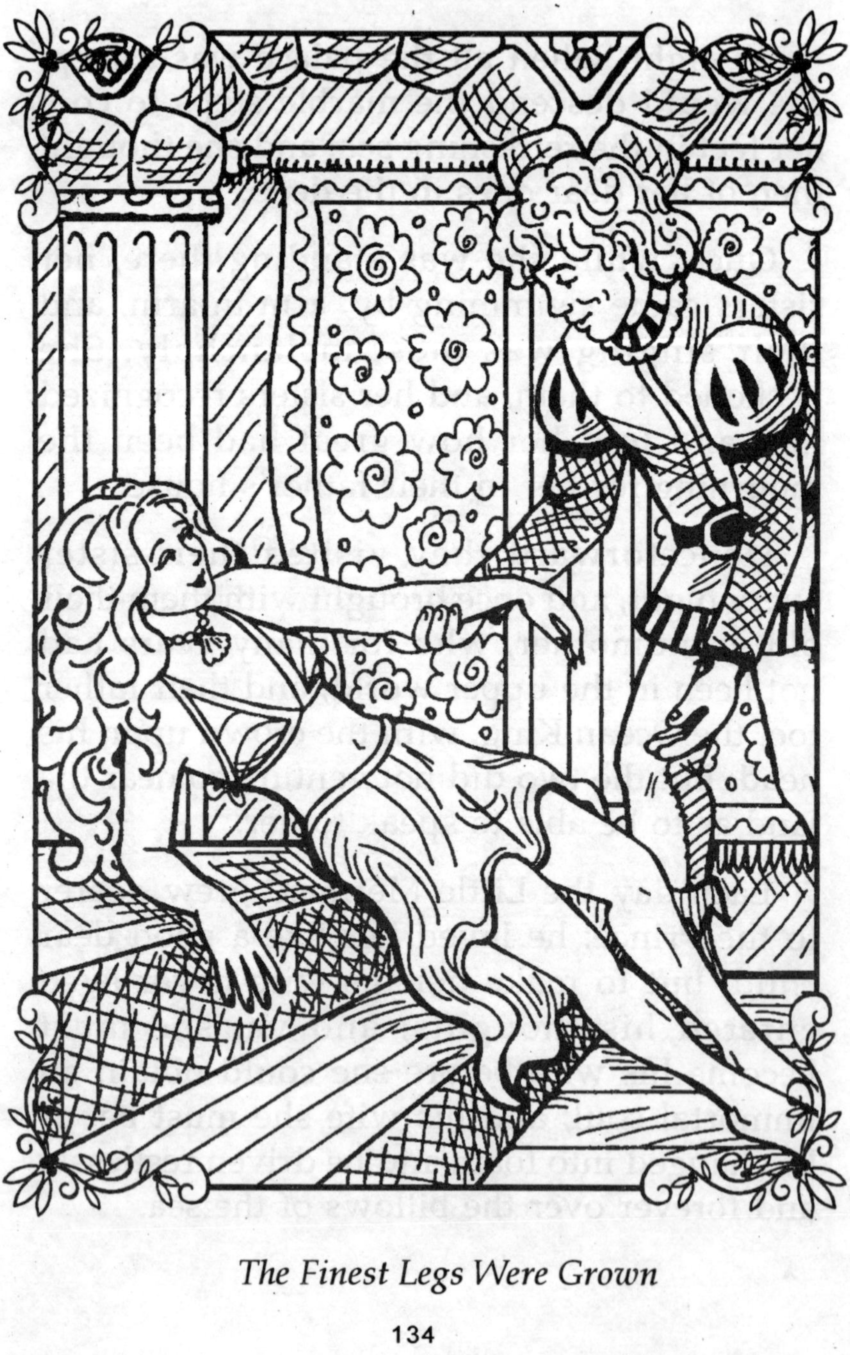

*The Finest Legs Were Grown*

"But do you not care most for me?" her eyes seemed to say.

"Yes," said the Prince, "you are dearer to me than all beside; for in goodness there is none like you. You are devoted and you resemble a maid that I once saw standing before me, but shall probably never behold again. I was on board a ship that was wrecked in a sudden storm; the waves threw me on the shore near a sacred temple, in which were many maidens. The youngest of them saved my life. I saw her but once; yet her image is vivid before my eyes – she is the only one I can ever love. But you are so like her – you almost drive her remembrance from me! But she belongs to the holy temple, and my good fortune has given me you as a consolation. Never, never will we be parted!"

"Oh, he does not know that it was I who saved his life!" thought the Little Mermaid with a sigh. "I bore him over the wild flood to the grove where the temple stands; I sat behind the rocks, and saw the beauteous maiden whom he loves more than me." And she sighed deeply at these words; for she could not weep. "She belongs to the holy temple, he says; she never goes into the world; she will never meet him again. But I am near him; I see him daily; I love him, and to him will I devote my whole life."

"The Prince will soon wed the daughter of our neighbor King," said the people: "and that's the reason why the stately ship is being got ready. 'Tis true, they say he is going to travel through the country; but the real reason is to see the Princess. That is the cause of his taking such a large retinue with him." But the Little Mermaid laughed at these conjectures; for she knew the Prince's intentions better than any one.

"I must make a journey," said he to her; "I must go and see the beautiful Princess. My parents require me to do so; but force me to marry her – to bring her back as my betrothed – that they will never do. Besides, it is impossible for me to love the Princess; for she cannot be as like the lovely maiden of the temple as you are; and if I am to choose, I would rather take thee, my little silent foundling, with the speaking eyes!" And he kissed her, and then she dreamed a sweet vision of mortal happiness and of an immortal soul.

"You do not fear the water, my child?" asked he tenderly, as she stood on the splendid ship that was to convey him to the territories of the neighboring monarch.

And then he told her of storms at sea, and of calms, or rare fish that inhabited the deep, and what divers had seen below. But she smiled as his words: for she knew better than any mortal creature how it looked, and what went on, in the depths of the ocean.

In the moonlit night, when all on board slept except the man at the helm, she sat at the bow and looked over the ship's side into the sea. It seemed to her as though she could see her father's palace and her old grandmother with her silver crown, as she gazed down into the waters.

And then her sisters appeared upon the waves, looked at her with sorrowful expression, and stretched out their arms towards her. She beckoned to them, smiled, and would have told them by signs that she was happy; but just at that moment the cabin-boy approached, and the sisters dived down so suddenly that the boy thought the white appearance he saw upon the surface of the water was the foam of the sea.

*The Little Mermaid Stretched Out Her Arms*

The next morning the ship entered the harbor of the splendid capital of the neighboring King. The bells rang a merry peal, and the clarions sounded from the high towers, while the soldiers in the streets paraded with waving colors and glittering arms.

Each day brought with it some new festival. But the Princess had not yet arrived in the town: she had been educated in a convent far off, where she had been taught the exercise of all royal virtues. At last she came.

The Little Mermaid was curious to see her beauty; and she was forced to acknowledge that she had never on earth beheld more noble features. The skin of the Princess was so fair and delicate and from behind her dark lashes smiled a pair of deep-brown eyes.

"It is herself!" exclaimed the Prince, on beholding her. "Thou art she who saved my life when I lay senseless on the shore!

"Oh, now I am more than happy!" said he to his little foundling. "That which I never hoped to see fulfilled has happened. Thou wilt

*They Did Not Venture So Near the Land*

rejoice at my happiness; for thou lovest me more than all who surround me."

Then the Little Mermaid kissed his hand in her sorrow, and she thought her heart would break; for the dawn of his marriage-day was to bring her unavoidable death.

And again the church bells rang, and heralds rode through the streets and announced the approaching wedding of the Princess. Flames burnt out of silver vases on every altar; bride and bridegroom gave each other their hands while the clergyman blessed the holy union.

The Little Mermaid, clad in silk and cloth of gold, stood behind the Princess and held the train of her bridal dress; but her ear heard not the solemn music, and her eye saw nothing of it. She flung herself into the sea, and she felt her body gradually dissolving into foam.

And the Little Mermaid stretched her transparent arms upwards to the sun, and, for the first time in her life, tears wetted her eyes.

And on the ship all were rejoicing; she saw the Prince and his lovely bride, and watched

*"But You Are So Like Her!"*

how both sought after her. Sorrowfully they looked at the froth of the sea, as if they knew that she had plunged into the waves. Unseen she kissed the bridegroom's forehead, smiled at him, and then rose with the air, and soared high above the rosy clouds that floated so peacefully.

*Rich in Sons*

# THE HONEY PRINCESS

Once upon a time there was a King who had three sons. The eldest two were very much alike, tall, slender and much given to foolishness. But they were paid attention to while their youngest brother, small and fair, was not given much mind. Though rich in sons, the King was poor in land and other royal considerations. Therefore it was determined that the eldest two should set out into the world to make their fortunes.

Off they went, but not for very long. Their foolish and extravagant ways quickly led to their being completely without funds, not even the means to return home to their father and the poor kingdom.

The youngest brother begged his father to let him go out and find the missing Princes. The King resisted, having no great faith in

*Let's Pull it Down*

this boy, telling him he was hardly likely to be able to make his way in the great world when it was obvious that his brothers, older and wiser, had not. But the boy begged long and loud, and at last the King relented.

The young boy set out and wherever he went stories of his brothers' foolishness reached him frequently enough that he was able to find them very quickly. He begged to be allowed to join them, to find their fortunes, and make their way back home.

At first the brothers laughed at him, that he should think himself wise enough to succeed where they had not, but at last he prevailed, and the three went off together.

They hadn't gone long when they came to a giant anthill.

"Let's pull it down," said the eldest brother, "it will be great fun to watch them jump about and try to save themselves."

"No!" insisted the youngest brother. "They are good creatures who work hard and do no one harm. We should not disturb nor injure them."

*"No!" insisted the youngest brother*

At last the older brothers left off kicking at the ant hill, and the three of them continued. They had not gone very far, however, when they came to a large pond. "Look at those fine fat ducks!" exclaimed the second brother. "Come, let us catch and roast a pair and have ourselves a fine dinner."

The eldest brother was all for it, but again the youngest protested. "Leave them alone," he demanded of his elders, "we have no right to disturb them and take their lives."

He kept on until the others heeded him and they once more made their way.

A humming, buzzing noise soon caught their attention and they stopped before a large beehive.

The fragrance of sweet honey filled the air, and so plentiful was the output of the hive that the golden liquid flowed from it on all sides.

"What fun!" laughed one of the older brothers. "Let's set it aflame and get all the honey for ourselves!"

"No, no, we mustn't," explained the youngest brother. "The bees are good folk,

*"The Bees Are Good Folk"*

and do naught but pleasantness in the world. Let them do as they would, and let us go on our way."

At last he prevailed with his elders, and on they went.

Before long, the three brothers came to a castle which looked very fine. They passed by the out buildings and stables, where there were quartered many fine-looking horses; but nothing moved, for each of those noble steeds was made of marble.

There was no one to be seen, so the brothers made their way into the castle itself. From room to room they went, without seeing another soul. At last they came to a door which had three locks on the side, and a grill in the middle. Through this grill they were able to see into the next room.

There, at last, was somebody: a little dwarf sat at a table. The brothers banged on the door and shouted until at last the dwarf heard them and approached.

He said not a word, but motioned for them to follow him. He led them to a large marble table on which was set everything needed for

*The Three Tablets*

a beautiful dinner. The dwarf motioned to the brothers to sit and partake of this repast, which they gladly did, having walked from where they had seen the beehive until they came to this place, without stopping for food or drink.

When at last they had satisfied themselves at the table, the dwarf led each of them to a beautiful bedchamber, and so the three brothers past a most restful night.

The next morning, the dwarf led them to yet another room which contained yet another marble table; on this were laid three tablets which explained how the castle could be made disenchanted.

The eldest brother undertook the first task. The tablet had foretold that in the castle garden, under the soil, lay a thousand missing pearls that belonged to the King's daughter. If they could be found before sunset, the finder would both bring the castle back to life, and marry the King's daughter. But if he should fail, he himself would be turned to marble.

The eldest brother searched in the garden all day, but by the time the sun was setting

*The eldest brother undertook the first task*

had found only the first hundred of the scattered pearls, and as the sun was disappearing over the hills, its last rays shone upon him, now another marble ornament in the garden where he had been standing.

The next brother sought to complete the task on the following day, but he did no better; he found the second hundred pearls only, and became himself marble.

When it was the youngest brother's turn, he looked hard and long, but the task was so difficult, especially for one as young and small as himself. He looked so hard and dug so deep that all his bones were aching, and at last he sat down on a large stone to rest himself.

As he sat there, along came an entire army of ants, the very ants that he had saved from his brothers' destruction.

"We have come to help you," said the King of the five thousand creatures, and before long all the pearls were heaped up in front of the youngest brother.

The dwarf was pleased enough, but then there was the next task to be fulfilled: the key

*The Missing Gold Key*

to the Princess's bedchamber had been lost in the moat, and must be fished out of it again.

As the youngest brother looked down into the bottomless-appearing water, he spied two ducks, the very ones he had kept his brothers from roasting and eating. They recognized him as well, and were only too glad, upon his instructions, to turn their broad bills toward the muddy bottom and bring up the missing gold key.

When the youngest brother presented it to the dwarf, he still remained silent, only smiling and pointing with his finger to the tablet with the third, and most difficult, task of all. And this was it: The King had three daughters, all beautiful and very much alike. The eldest had eaten a tiny piece of candy, the next one a lump of sugar, and the youngest a spoonful of honey. It was the task to guess, and to win, the Princess who had eaten of the honey.

A drone and a hum was heard in the castle, and through an open window the Queen of the bees, whose hive had been saved from fire by the youngest brother, flew in with all of her tribe behind her.

*She Could Tell at Once*

She, of course, could tell at once which Princess had eaten the honey. She buzzed and flew about her, so that the youngest brother could make his choice.

So the spell was broken, and all of the creatures who had been turned to marble woke from their slumbers and were alive again.

Even the two older brothers in the garden came back to their proper form.

Thus the youngest brother won his Princess, becoming the King's favorite, and succeeding him at last to the throne.

Gentle and forgiving in his nature, the youngest brother married off the elder two to his own Princess's sisters and all lived happily ever after in their new and prosperous kingdom.